Bella Tabbypaw

Daisy Meadows

ORCHARD

www.magicanimalfriends.co.uk

Friendship Forest

Ace Air Travel

Windmill

Mr Cleverfeather's Inventing Shed

Muddlepups' Den

Treasure Tree

Sparkly Falls

Featherbills' Barge

Waterwheel

Entrance to the Caverns

Swamp

Grizelda's Tower

Contents

PART ONE

Feline Friends!

CHAPTER ONE

A Golden Visitor

Lily Hart and her best friend, Jess Forester, were playing with four gorgeous kittens.

Lily's parents ran the Helping Paw Wildlife Hospital. Jess and her dad lived nearby. They had found the four kittens living in their garden shed!

"Jess saw a dog chasing a cat away from the shed," explained Mr Forester. "She hasn't come back yet, though."

Mr Hart checked all of the kittens. "If we keep them warm and give them milk they'll be fine," he said. He showed the girls how to feed the the kittens

with drops of milk from a
tiny pipette.

"I wonder who your mother
is," whispered Lily, stroking
one of the adorable kittens.
"It's a bit of a mystery. And we
already know one mysterious
cat, don't we, Jess?"

The two friends smiled,
thinking of their magical cat
friend, Goldie.

Goldie came from Friendship Forest, a secret world of talking animals. Lily and Jess helped Goldie to protect the forest from a mean witch called Grizelda. She wanted to get rid of the animals so she could have the forest to herself.

Just then the girls saw Goldie at the window. Jess grinned at her friend. "It must be time for another adventure in Friendship Forest!"

The girls followed Goldie to the magical Friendship Tree.

Jess and Lily held hands and said the magic words together: "Friendship Forest!"

A door appeared in the tree trunk. Jess and Lily followed Goldie through the door and found themselves in a sunlit clearing.

Goldie introduced the girls to Mr and Mrs Tabbypaw and Bella the kitten.

"Tonight I'm having a sleepover with Goldie!" said Bella. "Can you come too?"

Jess smiled. "Time stands still while we're here, so yes. A sleepover sounds fun!"

CHAPTER TWO

Strange Sounds

Bella's parents waved goodbye as the friends set off.

"Are those binoculars around your neck?" Lily asked Bella.

"These are night-vision goggles!" said the little kitten. "When I grow up I'll be able to see in the dark, like Goldie!"

They all sat down outside the Toadstool Café. Lily and Jess noticed that Goldie was looking worried.

"I heard some strange grunting sounds in the forest earlier today," explained Goldie.

Jess frowned. "Could it have been the Boggits?"

The Boggits were the mean and smelly servants of Grizelda the witch.

Just then there was a loud crash from inside the café. Mr and Mrs Longwhiskers were staring at a heap of saucepans on the floor.

"They were on the draining board a second ago," said Mrs Longwhiskers.

"Something very strange is going on in Friendship Forest!" Goldie said.

Next Goldie, Bella and the girls headed to Goldie's cosy grotto for the sleepover!

The friends curled up on the floor in quilts and soft cushions. Bella sat on Jess's lap.

"Will you tell me about the human world?" little Bella asked the girls.

So Lily told Bella all about the wildlife hospital, then Jess talked about school. Then it was Goldie's turn. "A legend says that deep beneath Friendship Forest are long-lost tunnels, full of sparkling jewels!"

Bella's eyes shone as she listened to the tale, but as soon as Goldie had finished talking the little kitten fell fast asleep.

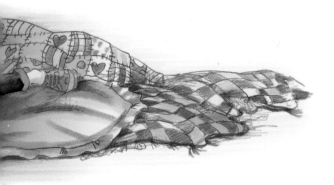

The three friends heard a strange sound outside and ran out to investigate. Jess spotted a dark, shadowy shape among the trees.

"I really hope Grizelda and her Boggits aren't back in the forest!" Lily said.

CHAPTER THREE

Footprints

The next morning, Lily woke first. But she couldn't see Bella anywhere, and her rucksack was also missing.

"Remember the noises we heard last night?" Lily asked. "Maybe Bella woke up and went to find out about them!"

The friends headed outside to search for Bella. They saw that it had rained heavily in the night.

At Toadstool Glade, Goldie jumped on to a log and called to all the animals. "Has anyone seen Bella Tabbypaw … or heard anything strange in the forest?"

A duckling wearing red wellies waddled forward. It was Ellie Featherbill!

"We saw footprints in the mud," Ellie said shyly.

Deep in the forest, Goldie
and the girls found four sets of
large footprints … and one set
of tiny pawprints.

"Only one kind of creature
could have made those big
prints," said Goldie. "Boggits!"

"The Boggits must have cat-napped Bella!" said Lily in dismay.

"Come on," said Jess. "We've got to get Bella back!"

The friends set off to follow the prints through the forest. Soon it began to rain again. Jess stopped and pointed. "Oh, no – the rain's washing the footprints away!"

Soon the friends weren't sure if they were going the right way any more.

"Where
can Bella be?"
Lily wondered aloud.
She looked around. "There
aren't that many trees here,
are there?"

"We're right at the edge of
Friendship Forest now!" cried
Goldie in alarm.

Lily pushed through some straggly bushes. Before her was a vast, oozing pool of mud. She gasped as her foot sank into the ground. "Help!" she cried. "I'm stuck in the swamp!"

PART TWO

The Secret Tunnels

CHAPTER FOUR

Boulder Barrier

"Lily! Hold on!" Jess cried.
She reached out a hand. Lily
clutched it, and together Jess
and Goldie pulled her free of
the swamp.

"Thank you!" Lily said.
"Now, let's get away from here
and find Bella."

The friends
spotted a big
footprint close to
a shady path. The
path took them past
stumpy trees and
across a leafy glade.

But soon they found their
way blocked by a heap of
huge grey boulders.

"This boulder is
shimmering!" cried Jess.
"Do you think it could
be magic?"

Goldie gasped. "Girls," she said excitedly, "I think we've found the entrance to the Friendship Forest tunnels!"

"But why would the Boggits go in there?" Jess wondered.

Lily frowned thoughtfully. "What if the strange noises were the Boggits snooping around?" she said. "They would

have heard Goldie
talking about
the jewels in the
tunnels!"

Jess nodded. "I think you're
right – they've decided to find
the jewels!"

"I'll go first," said Goldie. "I
can see in the dark!"

She held one end of her scarf
and Lily and Jess took the other
so they didn't get separated in
the dark tunnels.

The three friends crept along the tunnels. A loud noise echoed through the tunnels.

"Is that the Boggits?" Lily whispered.

The sound came again, closer this time …

CHAPTER FIVE

Glow in the Dark

Goldie and the girls pressed themselves against the cold tunnel wall.

Two shadowy shapes moved towards them.

"Hello!" said two little voices. It was a pair of cheeky-looking fox cubs.

"Girls," exclaimed Goldie, "meet Ruby and Rusty Fuzzybrush! But what are you two doing here?"

"We use the tunnels as our secret hiding place," said Ruby.

Goldie explained about Bella and the Boggits. "Will you help us find Bella?"

The fox cubs nodded eagerly.

"These special lanterns will help!" said Rusty.

Ruby put her mouth close to one of the lanterns and whispered, "Wakey, wakey, glow-worms. It's glowtime!"

Instantly, the lamp grew brighter until the tunnel was filled with blue light.

"Wow!" said Lily.

"It's magic!" She whispered to the glow-worms in the second lantern and it also lit up the tunnel with its bright glow.

Suddenly, a
gruff shout echoed down
the tunnel.

"Boggits!" said Goldie,
clutching at Jess and Lily.

"I'm so worried about
Bella!" said Lily, "Rusty
and Ruby, please
take us through
the tunnels so
we can
look for
her."

The foxes
darted away and
the others followed
them. Jess noticed
that the light from the
lanterns was casting
huge shadows on the
tunnel walls.
"The fox
cubs' shadows
make
them
seem
like
giants!"

Lily and Jess peered around the cavern. There were large stone pillars stretching from ceiling to floor.

Then, to their surprise, Bella appeared, wearing her night-vision goggles and whistling happily!

CHAPTER SIX

The Pillar Plan

"At least Bella's OK," whispered Jess. "But what is going on?"

The friends dimmed the lanterns and hid beneath an overhanging rock so they could spy on the Boggits without being seen.

"Oi, cat," Pongo grunted to Bella, "tell Boggits where cracks are in pillars."

After a moment, Bella said, "This one's cracked."

Pongo bashed the pillar with a large stone.

Sniff chuckled. "Pussycat can see cracks with special goggles. Cracks get bigger!"

Bella was pointing

upwards.
"Will you help
me with the jewels now
I've helped you?"

Jess glanced up at the cave
ceiling and gasped. "There are
jewels in the cavern roof!" she
whispered.

"The legend was right!"
breathed Goldie.

"Bella must have left Goldie's
grotto to go exploring and
bumped into the Boggits,"
whispered Lily. "They've
tricked her into helping them!"

Whiffy gave another pillar a bash. "Boggits are right under Toadstool Glade. When pillars fall, animals' cottages fall to bits! Grizelda be pleased!"

Lily gasped. "This is Grizelda's most terrible plan yet! We've simply got to stop the Boggits and save the animals' homes."

Jess glanced at her lantern and smiled. "I've got an idea for scaring away the Boggits," she said. "We need to create a shadow monster."

"Brilliant!" said Lily. "But we mustn't scare Bella." She picked up a stone and threw it to the other side of the cavern. The Boggits heard it land and lumbered towards it.

In a flash, Lily darted out
and scooped Bella up. Then she
ran back behind the rock.

Goldie explained to Bella
that the Boggits had tricked
her into helping them with
their mean plan.

Bella was horrified. "We have
to stop them!"

PART THREE

Home, Stinky Home!

CHAPTER SEVEN

Monster!

Jess told Bella her plan. The kitten nodded and raced back out into the cavern.

"There's a Boggit-eating monster in these tunnels!" she cried.

The Boggits looked around the cave nervously.

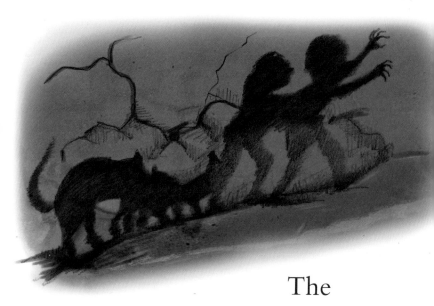

The
friends quickly made
themselves into the shape of
a scary monster.

Bella shone the lantern on
the friends, casting a huge
monster shadow on the wall.

"Aaaargh!" screeched Reek.

"Monster!" shrieked Pongo.
"Boggits run away!"

The friends chased the Boggits out of the tunnels and into the swamp outside.

The Boggits soon realised that they had been tricked … but they were so happy in the swamp that they didn't care.

"LOVELY mud!" shouted Reek, splashing around happily.

"The animals' houses are safe." Jess smiled. "Goldie, perhaps the Boggits can make their home here. That might stop them from causing any more trouble."

"Great idea!" Goldie agreed.
"But we'll need a bit of help!"

The cat fluttered her paws together. A moment later, clouds of butterflies arrived.

"Please ask the animals to come and help build the Boggits a home!" Goldie said.

CHAPTER SEVEN

Boggit Friends

Lots of animals arrived. Jess and
Lily helped Mr Cleverfeather
build a hut for the Boggits.
Pongo looked at it fondly, as
Sniff splashed in the mud. Reek
grunted, "Girls and cat help
Boggits. Girls are friends!"

Suddenly, there was a flash of light and Grizelda appeared, looking very angry!

"Lazy Boggits!" she screeched. "Smash those pillars!"

Pongo faced Grizelda. "Boggits not helping any more!" he shouted. "Boggits is happy here!"

Grizelda's

face was dark with rage. "I'll never give up," she snarled. "Friendship Forest will be mine one day!"

She snapped her bony fingers and vanished in a shower of red sparks.

The animals all cheered, "Hooray for the Boggits!"

Soon it was time for Lily and Jess to go home.

"We'll come back whenever we're needed!" said Lily and Jess, hugging their friend Goldie. She was sad to see them go.

The girls stepped through the door in the magical Friendship Tree and found themselves back in Brightley Meadow. As usual, no time at all had passed in their world!

Back at the wildlife hospital, the kittens were waking up. "The little one looks just like Bella Tabbypaw!" smiled Lily.

Jess's dad came back into the room. "I've been thinking, Jess ... Maybe we can keep one of the kittens?"

"Wow, thanks, Dad! I'd love

the little kitten!" Jess cried happily.

The best friends hugged the kitten and shared a secret smile. What a truly magical day!

The End

There's lots of fun for everyone at
www.magicanimalfriends.com

Play games and explore the secret world of
Friendship Forest, where animals can talk!

Join the
Magic Animal Friends Club!

Special competitions

Exclusive content

All the latest Magic Animal Friends news!

To join the Club, simply go to

www.magicanimalfriends.com/join-our-club/